For Mick, who isn't.
V.F.

For our grandparents.
R.A.

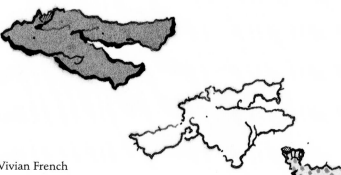

First U.S. edition 1995

Library of Congress Cataloging-in-Publication Data

French, Vivian.
Lazy Jack/retold by Vivian French ; illustrated by Russell Ayto.— First U.S. edition
Summary: A retelling of the misadventures of Lazy Jack who can never do anything right,
but people find his mishaps so funny that they employ him anyway
ISBN 1-56402-130-0
[1. Fairy tales. 2. Folklore—England.]   I. Ayto, Russell,   i11.
II. Title
PZ8.F897Laz 1995   398.2'0941'02—dc20   [E]

2 4 6 8 10 9 7 5 3 1

Printed in Hong Kong

The pictures in this book were done in watercolor and ink.

Candlewick Press
2067 Massachusetts Avenue
Cambridge, Massachusetts 02140

LAZY JACK

retold by
Vivian French

illustrated by
Russell Ayto

CANDLEWICK PRESS
CAMBRIDGE, MASSACHUSETTS

There was no one
as lazy as
Lazy
Jack.

He got out of bed in the afternoon

and he yawned   and he stretched

and he ate   and he drank   and he burped.

Then he went back to bed without ever
doing anything for anybody.

"This won't do!" said his mom.
"It just won't do!"
Jack went on snoring.
"This won't do at all!" said his mom,
and she went to ask the
builder to take Jack to
work with him.

The next day Jack

carried bricks   and buckets   and ladders

and wood   and cups of tea.

At the end of the day the builder thanked
him and gave him a coin.

Jack was pleased, and all the way
home he balanced the coin
on his thumb, on his finger,
on his head, and on his nose.
But it fell off his nose and
rolled into the bushes.

Jack was too lazy to look for it,
  so he went on home.
"Well?" said his mom. "Did you get paid?"
"I had a coin," said Jack, "but it
  fell off my nose and I lost it."
"Oh, Jack," said his mom.
    "You are a *silly* boy. You should have
      put it safely in your pocket."
Jack yawned. "I'll do that next time.
  May I go to bed now?"
His mom sighed and went to ask
  the farmer to take Jack
    to work with her.

The next day Jack

fed the cows   and the sheep   and the hens

and the pigs   and the ducks   and the geese.

At the end of the day the farmer thanked him
and gave him a big jug of milk.
"Don't spill it," said the farmer.
"I know what to do," said Jack. "My mom told me."
And he poured the milk into his pockets.
"There!" he said. "All safe!"

The farmer scratched her head
and walked away, and Jack
went hurrying home . . .

"Goodness me!" said his mom. "Whatever have you been doing?"

"Only what you said," said Jack. "The farmer gave me a jug of milk, so I put the milk in my pockets to keep it safe."

"Oh, Jack," said his mom. "You are a *silly* boy. You should have carried the jug home on your head."

Jack stretched. "I'll do that next time. May I go to bed now?"

His mom sighed and went to ask the dairyman to take Jack to work with him.

The next day Jack

swept the dairy and scrubbed the floor

and skimmed the milk and wrapped the cheeses.

At the end of the day the dairyman thanked him
and gave him a large wheel of cheese.
"It's sunny outside," said the dairyman.
"Be sure to keep your cheese cool."
"I know what to do," said Jack. "My mom told me."
And he put the cheese on his head and
walked out into the sunshine.

It wasn't long before the
cheese began to melt.
Jack wiped his face and
kept on walking . . .

Drip!
Drip! Drip! Drip!

"Heavens above!" said his mom.
"But I did what you said,"
said Jack. "I carried the
cheese home on my head."
"Oh, Jack," said his mom. "You
are a *silly* boy. You should
have wrapped it up in a wet
cloth to keep it cool."
Jack rubbed his eyes.
"I'll do that next time.
May I go to bed now?"
His mom sighed and
went to ask the
baker to take Jack
to work with him.

The next day Jack

mixed the dough   and kneaded the bread

and checked the ovens   and took out the loaves.

At the end of the day the baker thanked him.
"I keep a dog to catch rats," he said.
"Would you like one of her puppies?"
"Yes, *please*," said Jack, and he went to find a wet cloth.
"What's that for?" asked the baker.
"I know what to do," said Jack. "My mom told me."
And he tried to wrap up the puppy, but it
wriggled and tore his coat and ran away.

"Oh no," said Jack,
and he ran home to
his mom.

Mom!

"Hello," said his mom. "Why— your coat is all torn!"
"I did what you said," said Jack, "but the puppy didn't like the wet cloth."
"Oh, Jack," said his mom. "You are a *silly* boy. You should have tied a piece of string to its collar and let it walk beside you."
Jack nodded his head. "I'll do that next time. May I go to bed now?"
His mom sighed, and went to ask the fishmonger to take Jack to work with her.

The next day Jack

cleaned the counters   and tipped out the ice

and weighed the fish   and tied up the parcels.

At the end of the day the fishmonger thanked him
and gave him a huge silvery fish. "Would you like
some paper?" asked the fishmonger.
"I know what to do," said Jack. "My mom told me."
And he tied a piece of string around the fish and
began pulling it along beside him . . .

"What's this?" asked his mom.
"I did what you said," said Jack.
   "I tied the string around the fish and
      let it walk along beside me."
"Oh, Jack," said his mom.
   "You are a *silly* boy. You should
      have carried it home on your back."
Jack sighed. "I'll do that next time.
   May I go to bed now?"
His mom sighed too and made herself
   a cup of tea. Then she went to ask
      the grocer if he'd take Jack
         to work with him.

The next day Jack

sorted oranges   and apples   and pears

and loaded the cart   and drove around the town.

At the end of the day the grocer thanked him.
"I'm getting a pony to pull my cart," he said.
"You can have the donkey as your wages.
Do you want a rope to pull him with?"

"I know what to do," said Jack.
"My mom told me."
And he took a deep breath
and heaved the donkey
onto his back.

"*Whatever* is going on?" asked his mom,
   running to the gate.
  Jack put the donkey down and
     began to smile.
"I did what you said," he said proudly,
   "and brought my wages home."
"Oh, Jack," said his mom.
   "You are a *silly* boy."

But the grocer and the fishmonger and
   the baker and the dairyman and the
      farmer and the builder all shouted at once . . .

"He made me laugh more than I've ever laughed before," said the builder. "He can work for me every Monday, and I'll give him a coin."

And I'll put it in my pocket.

"He can work for me every Tuesday," said the farmer, "and I'll give him a jug of milk."

And I'll carry it on my head.

"He can work for me on Wednesday," said the dairyman. "I'll give him one of my best cheeses."

And I'll wrap it up in cool cloths.

"He can work for me on Thursday," said the baker, "and I'll give him as much bread as he wants—*and* the pick of the puppies."

"He can work for me on Friday," said the fishmonger, "and I'll make sure he has the biggest fish in the shop."

"Will you work for me on Saturday?" asked the grocer.
"I'll give you as many apples and oranges as you want."

And so he did!